Foodie Island

by
Dana Ryan

Illustrated by
Rosa C. Lopez

Foodie Island

The characters and events in this book are fictional, and any resemblance to actual persons or events is coincidental.

No part of this book may be reproduced or transmitted in any form or by any means, electronic or mechanical, including photocopying and recording, or by any information storage and retrieval system, without permission in writing from the publisher.

Cover design and illustration by Rosa C. Lopez.

Published by **Aqua tree**

An imprint of **Finca Books**

Copyright © 2019 Dana Ryan
All rights reserved.
ISBN: 978-1-7322574-5-0

For Jonas, who asked me to tell him a story.

D.R.

To you, the reader –
May your days be filled to the brim with fun adventures.

R.C.L

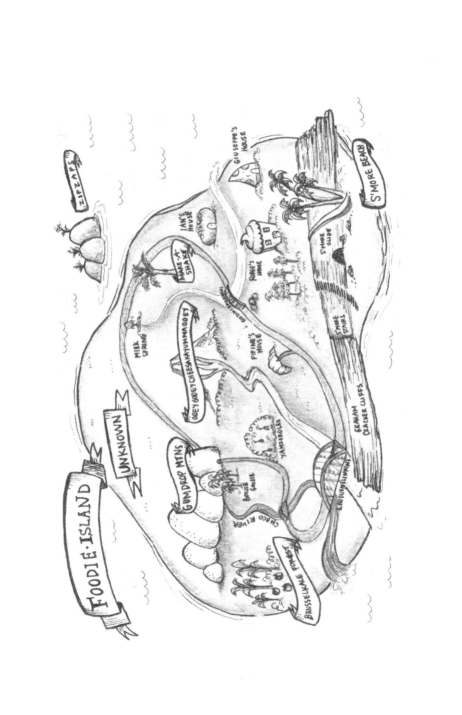

CONTENTS

	Explanations & Acknowledgments	i
1	The Bubble	1
2	An Elephant-sized Harrumph	6
3	A Deafening Pursuit	10
4	The Zipzaps and A Beavercoon	13
5	S'more Beach	18
6	The Chocolate Wafer Stairs	21
7	Rodge's House	25
8	A Delicious Tour	29
9	The Garage	34
10	Driving Lessons	38
11	Absolutely Gobsmacked	42
12	The Island	47
13	Boojiegoojies	52
14	Bouncing Boojiefruits	57
15	The Rescue	61
16	Joie de Jeanine Pie	64
17	An Explosion	69
18	Home Again	74
*	The How-To-Understand-Rodge Guide	81
**	Rodge's Ridiculous Rhymes	83

EXPLANATIONS & ACKNOWLEDGMENTS

When my 3-year-old asked for a story at bedtime, I snuggled down next to him and fabricated a short make-believe tale about an island. He begged to hear more the next night and the next and the next. And so, Foodie Island began to take shape, in spite of extreme parental fatigue, urgent emails and piles of laundry. What began as a simple request has become a much loved destination in our family's imagination. We hope it is the same for you. Because urgent emails and piles of laundry tend to stick around, but snuggly bedtimes with curious, cuddly children…alas, do not.

Thanks go to my oldest child, of course, for asking me to tell him a story. I am also grateful to his younger siblings, whose enthusiasm for the adventure encouraged me to write it down. My dear friend Meg van Heerden, somehow edited the manuscript shortly after giving birth to her fifth child while homeschooling the other four. Rosa Lopez has once again displayed her uncanny ability to take the stories in my head and bring them to life with her whimsical illustrations. And my husband, Daniel, continues to support my various artistic pursuits with enthusiasm, helpful advice and countless bars of dark chocolate.

1
THE BUBBLE

The last day of second grade felt like a sixty-foot long boa constrictor to Jesse Martin. All he could think about was sleeping in, staying in his pajamas all day, and putting together the new LEGO sets his grandparents had bought him for his birthday. When the last bell rang he leapt from his seat, said goodbye to his teacher, and ran out the door.

On the way home, Jesse's mother, Christy, pulled into a Sonic parking lot. Then she smiled and said, "Ice cream anyone?"

They had started the tradition when Jesse was in kindergarten. Now they always got soft serve on the last day of school. And, as usual, the final day was a scorcher. Jesse, his little brother, Zack, and their little sister, Avery, pressed their faces against the windows as a teenaged girl sailed to their car on roller skates. She handed over the ice cream cones and the race to eat the ice cream before it melted began.

"Was it a good last day?" Christy asked.

"Now it sure is!" Jesse said, smiling.

"And for you, Mr. Kindergartner?" Christy asked Zack.

Zack looked at her, gave himself an ice cream moustache and then flashed an impish grin. She laughed.

"Me like!" Avery said, her face a sticky mess.

Christy laughed again. She seemed bubbly, exhilarated. Jesse wasn't sure if it was the sugar, the three smiling faces, or the prospect of not doing school pick-ups and drop-offs for the next nine weeks…maybe all three. "I'm so excited about the summer!" his mom blurted. Then she paused. She appeared on the verge of happy tears, "Who knows what adventures we'll have?"

That night they had meatballs with spaghetti. Jesse watched as Zack tried to hide two green beans under his plate. Avery ratted him out. She kept pointing at Zack's plate and screaming. Zack's father, John, finally picked up Zack's plate in a last ditch effort to silence her.

"Well what do we have here?" John asked.

"Weird," Zack said, "I wonder how those got there?" He poked a cold string bean with his finger.

"Indeed," John said as he added two more beans to Zack's plate.

"Now I have to eat four?" Zack asked.

"Yes," John said.

"Can I have some ketchup?"

"Certainly."

Half a cup of ketchup later, Zack Martin managed to get all four green beans down without retching. Meanwhile, Avery covered her entire highchair and face in marinara sauce. Jesse watched half-admiring and half-grimacing as she did so. Once everyone had finished, Christy eased Avery from her chair before whisking her away for a bath. Jesse cleared his plate, squeezed soap into the sink and started the water while his dad cleared the table. And then they were all gone.

Jesse stood in front of the sink, wishing his mom would just use paper plates all the time like Michael's mom did. Michael was one of his school friends and he never had to wash dishes. It wasn't that Jesse minded washing dishes so much, it was just that lately he felt he kept doing the same things over and over. He wanted a change. He was tired of all the old familiar things. He wanted something different, new…exciting.

Through the open window he could hear his dad and younger brother, Zack, playing outside. Zack's chore was taking the kitchen scraps out to the compost bin. It took less time than washing dishes and then he always got to play outside afterward. Of course filling the compost had been Jesse's job when he was five too, but now that he was eight he had to do hard chores. And the only thing Avery had to do was fill her diaper, toddle around and make messes, all of which she did very well. Jesse looked at her dirty dinner plate and frowned. He loved spaghetti and meatballs; in fact they were his favorite dinner, but he disliked what Avery did to her plate when they ate them.

With a sigh, Jesse turned off the water and grabbed a dish towel. Then he reached for Avery's plate and plunked it into the soapy sink. As it sank, something odd happened. A bunch of bubbles flew up into the air and when Jesse reached out to touch the largest one, his finger went into the bubble, but it didn't pop.

At first Jesse didn't know what had happened. He felt a little funny, like he'd just gone upside down on a rollercoaster. But once that feeling passed, Jesse opened his eyes and looked around. He felt strange, but wasn't sure why. Then he looked down and instead of seeing the floor, he saw the sink filled with soapy bubbles. It was as if he were suspended above the sink!

Feeling disoriented, Jesse looked up. He saw the ceiling. He looked down again and saw the sink filled with soapy bubbles. He felt confused and unsettled. And then he noticed something curious. The faucet, the sink and the window looked much larger than normal as though everything had grown, or perhaps, as though he had shrunk.

2
AN ELEPHANT-SIZED HARRUMPH

A gust of wind blew in from the open dining room window and Jesse felt himself lift up into the air before sailing out the kitchen window. He fell off his feet and landed on a bouncy, somewhat sticky surface. He looked around. He seemed to be in a clear ball of some sort. He put his hand against the side of the ball and pushed. It bulged out where he pressed, but when he pulled his hand away, it sprang right back. It smelled clean and fresh and kind of like dish soap. *I think I'm in a bubble!* Jesse thought, *Yes! I'm actually inside a bubble!*

Then he noticed he was rising higher. As he peered down on his hands and knees, he watched his house become smaller and smaller. *I must be a hundred feet up in the air!* he thought.

A sudden breeze blew from the east. Propelled by the wind, the bubble began picking up speed. Jesse passed over the playground, the grocery store, and the library. And then he was above the freeway! In no time at all he flew over a mound of green dotted with pink and he realized the pink dots were flamingoes at the zoo.

"Hey you stinky flamingoes! I can finally look at you without smelling you!" Jesse yelled laughing.

Then he floated over the tall skyscrapers of downtown, his dad's workplace, and the harbor with its ships bobbing up and down like bath toys.

And then it grew very quiet. Almost eerily quiet. Jesse looked at the city behind him. Then he looked down and realized he was floating over a giant expanse of water. He was flying over the ocean! Jesse's heart thumped in panic and all he could think was, *What if the bubble pops? Would hungry sharks find me? Would the*

Coast Guard find me? Would ANYONE find me? After all, no one knew where he was, did they? Jesse tried to keep still. He imagined he was a statue and took slow, even breaths. He felt an itch on his right ankle, which he ignored. Then his left eye began to twitch, but he ignored that too.

Then suddenly a pelican flew right next to the bubble. Jesse stared, wide-eyed at the enormous bird. His eyes traveled down its giant gray-brown body and then back up to its razor sharp bill. He sat motionless and absolutely TERRIFIED. *Maybe,* he thought, *if I don't move, he won't try to eat me.* The pelican continued to fly without noticing Jesse. And he wouldn't have noticed the bubble if Jesse hadn't sneezed.

Jesse felt the sneeze coming with a sense of dread. He told himself he didn't have to sneeze. He tried to hold it in. But as the need to sneeze grew, Jesse could tell it wasn't going to be just any kind of sneeze, but that it was going to be a large, ear-splitting, elephant-sized kind of harrumph. And so, instead of trying to hold it in, Jesse decided to do the next best thing. When that big old sneeze finally frizzled up Jesse's nose he threw his head back and bellowed a giant, "ACHOOO!!!" right at the pelican.

The bird pulled up with a giant squawk, sending its feet over its head in a series of mid-air somersaults. Then it gave a strangled cry and plummeted downward.

When Jesse stopped laughing, he sat up and noticed a dark spot on the horizon. He stared at it, curious. As he watched, the dot grew larger and larger as the bubble continued to drift westwards. It changed from a black spot to a green and brown mound.

"It's an island!" he said. He pressed his hands against the bubble and watched as a sandy beach appeared. It was then that he realized he was descending and that he was, in fact, going to land on the island.

3
A DEAFENING PURSUIT

Jesse only had a moment to wonder who or what he might find on the island before, "*Pop!*" No longer in the bubble, he now stood on a wide sandy beach. A clump of palm trees stood to his right. Behind the trees stood a wall of tall, brown cliffs. There seemed to be a series of stairs from the beach to the top of the cliffs. So the island was inhabited. But by whom?

Before Jesse could answer that question, he heard a loud whooping sound. He turned in the direction of the sound and saw a furry creature running directly towards him.

"Run!" the creature yelled. It sped past Jesse and continued toward the stand of palm trees.

Jesse watched it run by and wondered why it was in such a hurry. And then Jesse heard them. It started as a hum, then grew into a roar of vibration. He looked up as a huge flock of bird-like animals shot over the cliffs and then dived down toward the beach. The noise was deafening. Jesse ran.

He sped toward the trees, looking over his shoulder and then scanning for a place to hide. The furry creature that had passed him was just reaching the stand of palm trees and Jesse watched it leap over a shiny, brown boulder and disappear. Jesse looked back. The birds were getting closer. Louder and louder, they sped towards him. He sprinted faster than he had ever sprinted before in his life. His lungs heaved. His legs burned. Sweat poured down his face. The birds neared. Then he slipped and fell hard on the sand.

He scrambled to get up, his feet scattering sand. With a fearful glance he saw the birds almost on top of him now, their raucous noise hammering his head. Still he ran, his heart pounding. He was within reach of the boulder now. He could see the spot where the furry creature had leapt over it. Then with a final burst of speed he threw himself over the boulder where he landed on a bed of sand and rolled once, then twice before everything went black.

4
THE ZIPZAPS AND A BEAVERCOON

"That was quite a debut!" the furry creature said.

Jesse opened his eyes. He was in a shallow cave and the animal was grinning at him. The creature appeared to be a mix between a raccoon and a beaver with a face and hands like a raccoon, but with big teeth and a tail like a beaver. Jesse sat up, wiping sand from his sweaty face. Some got in his mouth and tasted strangely sweet.

Jesse had grown up listening to and reading many fairy tales so the fact that a beavercoon was talking to him, and in a cockney accent no less, didn't seem the least bit strange. What did seem strange to him, however, was sand that tasted like graham cracker crumbs.

"It's sweet," Jesse said.

The animal looked at him oddly. "O' course it's sweet. What else would it be?" He peered at Jesse.

"Where am I?"

"This is Foodie Island."

"Foodie Island?"

"Yeah, Foodie Island, you know, where everfing's edible."

"Everything?"

"Far as I know," it said scratching its head. "O' course some parts o' the island I've never been to and I've just 'eard tales about what might be on the other side of Ooeygooeycheesakayummaooey, but I fink it's mostly fiddle faddle and," the animal suddenly stopped, looking somewhat abashed. "'Ere I go ramblin' on and on wivout even takin' the time to be polite. I'm Roger, but everyone calls me 'Rodge'." Rodge extended his right paw, which Jesse shook.

"Nice to meet you Rodge. I'm Jesse."

"First time to the island?"

"Yeah."

"Well," Rodge said, peering out of the shallow cave they were in, "'opefully the zipzaps will give up soon so I can show you around a bit."

"Zipzaps?"

"Yeah, zipzaps, you know, those birds what were chasin' us. They're crazy 'bout seek and 'ide."

"Don't you mean hide and seek?"

"No, I don't." He looked at Jesse with wide eyes. "You mean you don't know 'ow to play seek and 'ide?"

"Well, I mean…"

"You know, the game where you look for someone and then they have to 'ide." Rodge gave Jesse a quizzical look. "Kid doesn't know seek and 'ide," he mumbled under his breath. "Can't even imagine."

"What happens once they hide?"

"That's it."

"So they just stay there hiding?"

"Yeah, until it's safe to come out." Rodge shook his head and mumbled. Snippets of phrases like "can't believe" and "seek and 'ide" and "poor little tyke," could be heard under his breath.

"But what if you come out and they find you again?"

"Well then you 'ide again o' course!"

"So how do you win?"

"Win? Win?! Who said anyfing about winnin'?"

"Well, if nobody wins, then what's the point?"

"The point? The point?!" Rodge stopped and scratched his head. "Hmmm…that's a very good question, young man. I'll 'ave to ask the zipzaps."

"So the zipzaps aren't dangerous?"

"The zipzaps dangerous? Why…why..." and Rodge began to chuckle. Then he started to shudder and shake until he finally exploded into a fit of raucous, booming laughter. He fell onto the cave floor and held his heaving sides. Then he flipped onto his stomach and pounded his fists and tail on the ground while gasping for breath. Tears streamed from his eyes.

    Jesse sat on a smooth rock, a wry look on his face. "I take it they're not?"

    Rodge sat up, tried to recover himself and then dissolved again into shaking laughter. And even though he was laughing at Jesse's expense, the sound of Rodge's laughter was so infectious that Jesse couldn't help smiling. Finally Rodge calmed down. He sighed as he wiped his eyes and cheeks with his paws.

    "Ahhh, now that was delightful!" Rodge said, his face rapt. "I 'aven't laughed that 'ard for quite a while."

    "Glad I could help you out," Jesse said dryly.

"To answer your question," Rodge said, attempting a serious look, but failing, "the zipzaps are the most playful, colorful, social, creative and unbelievably noisy birds you've ever met, but they are certainly not dangerous."

"And the goggles?"

"What about 'em?"

"Why do they have goggles on?"

"That, my boy, is just one o' the many great mysteries of the zipzap."

5
S'MORE BEACH

They sat in silence for a few moments. Then Rodge held his finger to his lips, or rather, to his large, beaver teeth, and crept to the mouth of the cave. He peered out. Then he motioned for Jesse to come closer. Jesse tiptoed to the cave entrance. Rodge pointed to a small bird perched on one of the shiny rocks.

"A zipzap?" Jesse whispered.

"Yes. They're gregarious in groups, but extremely shy when alone."

Jesse stared at the bird. It reminded him of the parrot that his friend Jack had as a pet. But the coloring was different. As the eye traveled from the head to the tail feathers, the colors changed from dark navy to turquoise to emerald to lime green. The feet and beak were a brilliant orange. And emerging from its back were two bright yellow feathers that hung limp and long. But the most startling thing about the bird was the fact that it was wearing goggles. They looked like the kind of goggles worn by fighter pilots. And they made the zipzap's eyes appear large, as though it viewed the world through magnifying glasses.

As Jesse watched the bird, it began pecking at the shiny rock. Shards of dark brown flew into the air.

"What's it doing?" Jesse asked, his voice low.

"Gettin' a snack most likely."

"It eats rocks?"

"They're good. You should try 'em."

Rodge walked out of the cave and the zipzap, upon seeing him, stopped pecking. Then it saw Jesse. The bird's eyes grew even larger and the two long yellow feathers on its back immediately straightened. Jesse watched with fascination as the feathers began to rotate like helicopter blades. They whipped faster and faster until the bird lifted up and sped away into the sky.

Jesse stared in amazement. "That was the most incredible thing I've ever seen!"

Rodge broke a piece off the shiny rock and brought it over to Jesse.

"'ere," he said, "give it a go."

Jesse stared at the chunk of rock, shrugged and took a bite. As he chewed, a large smile spread across his face. "It tastes just like a chocolate covered malt ball!"

"As it should," said Rodge, "all the rocks taste like that on S'more beach."

"S'more beach?"

"Yup, this 'ere's S'more beach…graham cracker sand, chocolate rocks and those flowers over there, the big white puffy ones, taste just like marshmallow. And that's why we 'ave all our bonfires on this 'ere spot."

"Who's we?"

"All the animals 'o course!"

"There are more of you?"

"Lots more! Although not as many as there used to be." Rodge looked sad.

Just then Jesse's stomach rumbled loudly.

"Sounds like you need a proper meal," Rodge said, "Next stop, my 'ouse."

6
THE CHOCOLATE WAFER STAIRS

Jesse followed Rodge as he led them across the beach and toward a set of stairs. When they got to the bottom of the stairs, Jesse looked up. He saw a long, zigzagging network of steps ascending the tall cliffs.

"You have to climb *all* those steps just to get to your house?" Jesse asked.

"Yup," Rodge said, "all 365 of 'em."

"365? That's like a…a…"

"A step for every day o' the year? Right. And it's a good reminder to be grateful for each one…especially when you make it to the top or bottom. At least, that's what my friend Ian says."

"Ian?"

"Nice chap, even though he reads too much and likes classical music. Sometimes I call him 'The Professor.' Ian's not, mind you, but some people just look like they'd enjoy typing up a syllabus."

"A silly-what?"

"Never mind…I'm just prattlin' on."

Jesse looked down at the next step and then stopped. He reached down to knock on it.

"Are these…?"

"Chocolate covered wafers," answered Rodge. "They're some o' my favorites."

Jesse stared down in amazement.

"Go on," Rodge said, "take a bite."

"Take a bite?" Jesse hesitated, "But...if I eat some of the step, won't it ruin the stairs?"

"Try it," Rodge said. Then he smiled a strange, twinkling smile.

Jesse reached down and broke off a piece of the step. He put it in his mouth. The mixture of chocolate and crunchy wafer was delightful. "Yum!" he said. He looked down at the step where he had broken off a piece. The stair looked perfect. "How…how did it do that?" he asked amazed.

Rodge shrugged. "It just does. It all does on Foodie Island, although 'public use' areas grow back more quickly."

"But how?"

"It's just the way tis."

Jesse's stomach grumbled again.

"On we go! Just two 'undred fifty more steps and we'll be at the top."

They dropped into a companionable silence. The sea glittered behind them as they climbed up the crisscrossing stairway. Jesse noticed how the cliffs resembled graham crackers stacked one on top of the other and they reminded him of limestone cliffs. The breeze carried sweet scents of malted chocolate, sugary marshmallow, and honeyed graham cracker. Jesse drank in great big gulps of air. And on his face, set between his two ears, sat the silliest, widest grin any eight-year-old boy ever had before or since. He kept thinking how washing dishes had turned out to be a pretty good chore after all.

When they reached the top of the stairs, they stopped for a minute to pant and huff and refill their lungs. Then they set off on a path thickly bordered by flowering shrubs, vines and grasses. Jesse recognized none of them, but assumed they were all edible. Rodge rushed along the path, leaving Jesse unable to sample anything and breathless to keep up. The jungle canopy closed tight around them. Light filtered through breaks in the trees overhead, but much of the path remained dark and Jesse feared becoming lost. Then all of a sudden, they emerged into a clearing. Rodge stopped so abruptly that Jesse nearly bowled him over.

"'ome sweet 'ome," Rodge said, pointing ahead.

Jesse looked up and his mouth fell wide open.

7
RODGE'S HOUSE

Towering in front of Rodge and Jesse was the biggest, most splendid looking cupcake that Jesse had ever seen. The brown cake blazed with streaks of orange, and on its rounded top sat a perfect spiraling swirl of cream colored icing. Its sugary edges flashed in the sun. The path led up to a door in the middle of the cupcake with two windows on either side.

"This…this is your house?" Jesse asked.

"Yup," Rodge smiled proudly. "I 'ad a cream filled doughnut for a bit, but I got simply whacked sloggin' through all that cream, so now I've got this one."

"And it's…"

"A carrot ginger cupcake with cream cheese frostin'. It's much cleaner. And the ginger 'as great 'ealth benefits."

"And it's...well…I mean, you can eat it? Your house I mean?"

"Why not? Not that I'd want to, or at least, not all at once. I take bites from the walls when I get 'ungry o' course or take a swipe o' frostin' from the roof now and again."

Jesse was grinning. He couldn't imagine being able to eat his house. In fact, the idea struck him as so deliciously funny that he began laughing.

"What is it?" Rodge asked.

"You…," Jesse couldn't stop laughing, "you…you can eat your wall?!" Jesse sputtered.

"Well, yeah," Rodge said, "or a chair, or a sofa, or even a bed."

"A chair!" Jesse blurted, still laughing.

"And some people," Rodge glanced around before lowering his voice to a whisper, "'ave been known to eat their front doors, but I've never been quite that 'ungry."

"Their front doors?!"

"Some doors *are* pretty scrumptious."

Jesse doubled over. His whole body shook as he laughed. Rodge gave him a quizzical look and waited. And then waited some more.

Wiping tears from his eyes Jesse finally stood and said, "Whew! I haven't laughed that hard for quite a while."

"'appy to oblige you," Rodge said and they grinned at one another. "Would you like a look see?"

"A what?"

"A bit of a…you know…a look 'round?"

"Oh, yes please!"

Rodge walked ahead on the path and Jesse followed him. A cluster of flowers grew in front of the house. They looked wild and untended, with long narrow leaves and puffy pink flowers. Jesse stared at them.

"Try one," Rodge said.

Jesse bent down and picked a flower, but when he stood up, a sudden breeze blew the pink puffs into the air. They reminded him of dandelions. He picked another one

and slowly brought it to his mouth. The pink puffs dissolved on his tongue. "It tastes like cotton candy, but…but made from blackberries!"

Rodge smiled, "They were me mum's favorites. So I'm a bit soft'earted about 'em you might say." Rodge opened his front door and held it open for Jesse to enter. As Jesse walked closer to the house, the smell of gingery cinnamon grew stronger and stronger. He inhaled deeply. It was like standing outside a bakery. Then he walked through the cupcake's door.

8
A DELICIOUS TOUR

The first thing Jesse noticed was the brightness. He had expected the inside of a cupcake to be somewhat dim, with a spongy, closed in sort of feeling. But Rodge's house was bright and open and airy. And it smelled fantastic.

The cupcake floor felt soft and springy under Jesse's feet, rather like a plush carpet. He jumped and the floor sent him bouncing up and down.

"This is so cool!" Jesse said.

"Is that a good fing?" Rodge asked.

"What? Being cool?"

"Yeah."

"Well," Jesse shrugged, "where I'm from it is."

"And if somefing's not cool, it's 'ot?"

Jesse laughed. "No, not hot. It's…it's hard to explain. But, maybe boring? If something's not cool it's not very interesting."

"A bit 'umdrum then?"

"I guess so."

"Well then, follow me and I'll show you somefing' 'cool'."

Rodge bounded ahead through the entryway and into a round opening. Jesse followed and found himself in a hallway just in time to see Rodge disappear through yet another round opening to the right. "Hey, wait up!" Jesse walked through the opening. A set of stairs led upwards. He bounced from stair to stair until he reached the top, and when he looked down, he saw Rodge grinning at him from the bottom of a long slide.

"C'mon," said Rodge. "Give it a go."

Jesse stepped onto the slide and let out a whoop as he hurtled downwards. He landed on a fluffy, pillowy mound that looked like a giant white cushion.

"Your bed?" Jesse asked.

"Yup. And that's 'ow I get in it every night."

Jesse looked down at the white mound of bed. "May I?" he asked and when Rodge nodded, Jesse grabbed a chunk of the mound and took a bite. "Angel food cake," he said grinning. "I don't think I'd ever get out of bed."

Rodge laughed. "'ere now, I know you're 'ungry. Let's go on and see the kitchen eh?"

Jesse slid down the side of the enormous, cushion-like bed and landed on the carrot cupcake floor with a springy bounce. He followed Rodge into a small, but bright and clean kitchen. And as Jesse stared at the countertops and cupboards, trying to figure out what they might all be made of Rodge said, "Try it. Try it all!"

Jesse walked around the room, breaking off pieces of the furnishings. He felt odd and thought of all the times his mother asked him to put a book beneath his paper when writing to keep from scratching the kitchen

table. Forget scratches, now he was breaking off or biting whole chunks out of the cupboards and counters!

He tasted sesame cracker cupboards, cheddar cheese counters, pretzel chairs, apricot cushions and even an Oreo cookie table. He especially liked the table.

"You're house," Jesse said with his mouth full of cookie, "is absolutely the most fantastic house I've ever been in."

"But I 'aven't even shown you the best part yet."
"What?!"
"Follow me!"

Jesse struggled to keep up as Rodge sped down the hallway. As Rodge passed a door on their left he yelled out, "Guest room!" and then, "Bathroom!" when they passed one on their right. Jesse wanted to see (and taste) everything (well, except maybe the bathroom), but Rodge plowed on until they reached a small door at the end of the hallway. He paused before turning the handle and smiled at Jesse. Then he gave the door a push and flung it open wide. Jesse stared in disbelief.

9
THE GARAGE

"Are they all…" Jesse asked.

"Mine?"

"No, I mean, yes, but, well, are they all, um, well, what are they?"

"What are they?! What are they?! Why they're motorcars of course! What else would I 'ave in my garage?"

"Well…it's just that I've never seen a hot dog car before, or…or a pickle one either."

"Ah, two o' the best."

"And that one there?" Jesse pointed to what looked like a blueberry muffin with half a top.

"That's my blueberry muffin motorcar. It's a convertible because I'm always eatin' off the top too fast for it to grow back. The top's the best part you know."

Jesse walked amongst the cars, passing an enormous grape, a peanut butter and jelly sandwich, a banana, a wedge of cheese, a carrot and even a hamburger! Jesse rubbed his eyes, wondering if maybe it

Foodie Island

was all just a dream. But when he opened his eyes again, the cars were still there in all of their strangeness. And he could smell them too, from the sweetness of the banana to the salty tang of the hot dog. It all felt so *real*. But could a place so wildly strange truly be real? Or was his desperation for something new in his life causing him to imagine odd places and to do even odder things?

"Jesse?"

"Yeah, sorry, I was just thinking."

"I try not to do too much o' that. Leave that sort o' fing to my friend, Ian."

Jesse smiled.

"So which one would you like?"

"You mean…"

"Yeah, pick whichever one you like, well, except maybe the 'ot dog. I just put in 'ydraulics and it's still a bit dodgy. But other than that, you can 'ave your pick of all the others. 'owever, you might swallow a few bugs if you drive the muffin motorcar and you'll get just a bit sticky in the grape car, but I'm workin' on that."

"Well," Jesse looked around at all the options, "the thing is…"

"Yes?"

"Well…," he scratched his head, "I don't know how to drive."

"Don't know 'ow to drive?!"

"No."

"'ow old are you?"

"Eight.

"And?"

"And eight-year-old boys don't drive where I'm from."

Rodge looked scandalized. "Not drivin' yet at eight-years-old?" Rodge contemplated this for a moment. "Well then, 'ow old must you be?"

"Sixteen."

"Sixteen?! What kind o' barbaric place is it? No drivin' till you're sixteen?! Unbelievable!"

"I think there's a general concern about safety and the ability to see over the steering wheel."

"Backwards I tell you," Rodge muttered under his breath. "Absolutely backwards." Rodge kept muttering to himself. When he finally stopped, an awkward silence settled over them. Jesse drew circles on the floor with his foot. Rodge cleared his throat.

"Well," Rodge said, "then I guess there's just one fing to do."

Jesse looked at him with puckered eyebrows.

"Young man, it's time you learned 'ow to drive."

10
DRIVING LESSONS

Rodge walked over to the hot dog car. "C'mon then."

Jesse followed Rodge, opened the passenger door and climbed in. Then suddenly, Rodge was standing next to the passenger door. He looked down at Jesse.

"Out." Rodge said.

"Out?"

"Yes. Out. 'ow can I teach you to drive if you're not drivin'?"

"Well, I thought…"

"Finkin' again, that's the problem. Stop finkin' and choose a motorcar please."

Jesse walked past the blueberry muffin convertible, lingered next to the banana, and stopped beside the pickle. He didn't really like pickles that much, but his mom did, especially when she had been pregnant with Avery. For some reason, seeing the pickle made Jesse think of her and of Avery and all of a sudden he felt tears in his eyes. He wondered what everyone was doing and if they were missing him. He hadn't been gone for that long, but surely they would have noticed by now, wouldn't they? Maybe Avery was asking for "Ebbie" (her name for Jesse) and Zack wanted to wrestle. Jesse smiled. Zack always wanted to wrestle.

"You in a pickle yet?" Rodge asked, then laughed.

"Almost," Jesse said as he climbed in.

The interior smelled faintly like vinegar, but not overpowering. The seats felt like alligator skin, or at least how Jesse imagined alligator skin might feel. He gripped the steering wheel and an odd sense came over him. A part of him felt guilty, like he was doing something wrong; the other part of him felt exhilarated.

A motor-like noise caught Jesse's attention and he looked up to see the garage door opening. Rodge started the hot dog and drove over to idle beside Jesse.

"You see that button next to the steerin' wheel?" he yelled into Jesse's window.

"The blue one?"

"Yeah. Push that and your motorcar will start."

Jesse reached out and pushed the blue button. The pickle jumped, sputtered once, twice, then let out an enormous, *Pop*! before rumbling to life. Jesse sat wide-eyed. Rodge roared with laughter.

"She's got quite a pop, eh?"

"Um, quite."

"Now you see the foot pedal on your right?"

"Yes. Let me guess, the gas pedal?"

"Gas, what's gas?"

"You know, how the car runs."

"I've no idea what gas is, but your car runs on pickle juice."

"And yours?"

"Ketchup and mustard, naturally."

"I can't believe it!"
"Well, you will when you step on that pedal."

Jesse put his foot on the pedal, just to see how it felt and gave a gentle tap. *Vroom!* The pickle shot out of the garage.

11
ABSOLUTELY GOBSMACKED

Later, Rodge told Jesse that at first he was too stunned to move. He just watched as Jesse picked up speed in a green blur. Then he gripped the steering wheel, stomped on the ketchup/mustard pedal and sped out of the garage in pursuit of the pickle.

"HELP!" Jesse wailed.

Rodge watched as the pickle car aimed straight for his neighbor Giovanni's house; an enormous wedge of ham, sausage and pepperoni pizza with extra cheese.

"Crank it!" Rodge yelled.

Jesse turned the car to the right.

"Not that way!" Rodge strained forward in his car, willing it to go faster.

The pickle careened toward the Graham Cracker Cliffs. The hot dog car sped after it.

"Stop!" Rodge screamed, but the pickle car still raced toward the edge of the cliffs. Rodge yelled again and again, but it was too late, and Rodge watched with horror as the pickle shot off the edge of the cliffs and disappeared.

Rodge couldn't believe it. He jumped out of the hot dog and ran to the cliff edge. And just as he peered over, he saw the pickle car, with Jesse still in it, plow into the top of a palm tree. Then the strangest thing happened. The tree, instead of snapping in two, bent way, way over and then, like a catapult, shot the pickle car back onto the cliff ridge. It landed right side up. And Jesse, who sat gripping the steering wheel with white knuckles, looked at Rodge with eyes the size of oranges.

Rodge walked to the pickle car, his beavercoon knees knocking. "Are you alright?"

"I'm…I'm…I think so."

"I'm absolutely gobsmacked! That was the most amazing fing I've ever seen!"

Jesse still sat wide-eyed, the steering wheel clenched in his hands. "I…I think it's maybe the most amazing thing that's ever happened to me…other than the bubble." A slow, wobbly smile spread across his face.

Then Jesse and Rodge both looked up as a car sped towards them. It drew up beside them before coming to a stop. It was driven by an animal with a hedgehog body and a squirrel-like tail who also happened to be wearing a bow tie and a gray, tweed cap. The round car resembled a biscuit with crumbly layers which were studded with some kind of dark, dried fruit.

"What kind of car is that?" Jesse asked.

"This," the hedgesquirrel said, exiting smoothly, "is a dried currant scone."

"Not a sconce?" Rodge asked with a mischievous smile on his face.

"No, it is not a light fixture…which you know very well."

"Jesse," Rodge said, "meet my friend, Ian. Ian, this is my friend, Jesse, and it's 'is first time to the island."

"It's a pleasure," Ian smiled.

"It's nice to meet you too," Jesse said.

"I heard a commotion as I was driving by and came to see what it was all about."

Rodge looked sheepish. "Well…I thought I would teach Jesse 'ow to drive seein' as he doesn't know 'ow and…well…"

"I drove off the cliff!" Jesse blurted.
"You what?" Ian asked, looking at Jesse.

"Yeah, I drove right over those cliffs there, landed on a palm tree, and it shot me like a slingshot up into the air and back here!"

"And all in one piece? I can hardly believe it!" Then Ian looked more closely at Jesse and said, 'You must have been terrified."

"It was…slightly...terrifying."

"Are you alright?"

"O' course 'e's alright," Rodge said.

"But he just drove off a cliff!"

"I know, but, look at 'im. Jesse's made o' nice, sturdy stuff. 'e's fine." Rodge paused as Ian looked at Jesse. "In fact, I bet 'e's ready to keep drivin'."

Jesse smiled weakly. "Well, I, uh, I think I might actually like to take a break."

"Here," Ian said, "why don't you jump in and I'll take you on a bit of a drive. Show you around a little."

Jesse exited the pickle and got into the scone. Rodge, grumbling, followed in his hot dog.

12
THE ISLAND

Ian eased onto a black road that looked a lot like Rodge's Oreo dining table and drove until they reached a signpost. The signs pointing to the right read, "Make-A-Shake Tree", "White Spring", and "Ooeygooeycheesakayummaooey". On the left, the signs read, "Brusselkale Forest", "Gumdrop Mountains", "Boojiegoojies", and "Ooeygooeycheesakayummaooey."

"Why does it have Ooeygooeychees-a-whatever-you-call-it, on both sides?" Jesse asked.

"That is an excellent question. And the answer is that either we're daft, or else there's a reasonable explanation. The reasonable explanation is that Ooeygooeycheesakayummaooey is the name of the volcano in the center of the island and since the island is more or less round, you can get to it from both directions."

"Oh. So you're not drafty, or, whatever you said."

Ian chuckled. "We're not daft...which means we're not crazy. Although you might think otherwise!"

Jesse laughed. He liked Ian. He turned around to look at Rodge and saw with astonishment that the hot dog was now six feet high in the air.

"'ydraulics!" Rodge yelled grinning.

When Jesse turned back around, Ian eased the car to the left. The ocean shimmered blue out Ian's window and Jesse watched the sunlight sparkle across the waves like iridescent gems. On Jesse's side of the car stood a green meadow, its grass-like stalks swaying lazily in the warm breeze. Then they passed a sign that read, "Linguinilinkini" and soon afterwards crossed a bridge straddling a dark brown river.

"That's the 'Choco River'," Ian said, "Starts way up somewhere in the Gumdrop Mountains and runs all the way down here."

"And it's made of…"

"Chocolate milk."

"Mmm…sounds delicious."

The road curved away from the ocean.

"That there," Ian pointed with his left hand, "is the Brusselkale Forest."

"That sounds…"

"Disgusting!" they both said at the same time. Then they looked at each other in surprise and burst out laughing.

They crossed another bridge.

"What are those strange bushes?" Jesse asked. He stared out the windshield at a cluster of tall green bushes with yellow flowers that resembled upside down goblets.

"Yamzirdles."

"Yam-whatty's?"

"Here, I'll pull over and you can try some. It's a lot easier than trying to explain." He pulled to the side of the road and slowed the scone to a stop. They walked together down a gentle slope until they reached the cluster of bushes. Ian reached up and tugged on one of the flowers.

The yellow goblet dropped into his hand, he turned it upright and handed it to Jesse. Jesse took the flower and peered inside. He saw a clear liquid, with tiny bubbles rising to the surface. He took a sip.

"It's delicious!" And indeed it was. Later Jesse described it as a sweet, but not overly sweet, bubbly and refreshing drink that reminded him faintly of pink lemonade.

"It's called 'yamzirdy.' The drink I mean. The bushes are yamzirdle bushes, but the drink is called yamzirdy."

"I'd call it yamyummy!"

Ian reached up to grab a flower for himself, but just as he did so, a loud cry rang out. He stopped.

"HELP!" The cry came again.

"That's Fifine!" Ian said.

"Fi-who?"

"Come on! She's in trouble!" And he raced toward the scene. Jesse grabbed a second flower for the road and followed Ian, the liquid sloshing over the sides of the goblet as he ran.

13
BOOJIEGOOJIES

Rodge, who was still seated six feet off the ground in his hot dog car said, "It came from the boojiegoojies!"

Images of monsters instantly popped into Jesse's head. He pictured someone being held captive against his or her will, trapped by purple hairy beasts with green eyes and orange horns. And he thought, maybe he didn't like Foodie Island after all. Everything might taste great, but if there was something lurking out there that thought *he* tasted great, well, maybe he'd had enough. He slowed to a jog.

"C'mon!" Ian yelled.

The scone car began to move forward. And then, realizing that if he didn't hurry up he might be left behind to face the boojie-whatever-they-were on his own, Jesse threw his head back, gulped the yamzirdy juice and yelled, "Wait for me!"

With a leap, Jesse managed to get into the rolling scone before it roared down the road. They hurtled toward a stand of trees. And the closer they got, the

stranger the trees appeared. The trunks of the trees were dotted with small ledges, as though it grew natural hand and footholds for people to climb. Broad leaves sprouted from the trunk at the top, much like the leaves on a banana tree. But this tree, instead of growing bananas, grew bright red ovals that dangled down on long vine-like growths. Sun sparkled through the translucent ovals making the entire stand of trees appear ablaze.

"What are they?" Jesse asked as Ian pulled the scone to the side of the road.

"Boojiegoojie trees," he said.

"Oh," Jesse said with relief, "I thought they were…"

But Jesse never finished because the cry for help sounded once again.

Rodge pulled over in his elevated hot dog, pointed and said, "She's on the Toffee Rocks!"

"Let's go!" Ian said.

Ian set off toward the cluster of trees and Jesse followed. Rodge didn't move. Ian looked back at Rodge.

"Aren't you coming then?" Ian asked.

Rodge looked at Ian sheepishly.

"Your hydraulics are stuck aren't they?" Ian asked.

"Maybe."

Ian started laughing. Rodge pretended not to notice.

"Remember what I said about putting hydraulics in your hot dog car?"

Rodge acted as if he didn't hear.

"Leave your buttocks alone, I said!"

"It's not buttocks!" Rodge sputtered. "It's buns! You put 'ot dogs in buns. You DO NOT put them in buttocks! You…oh never mind!" Rodge threw up his hands in frustration.

The spines on Ian's hedgesquirrel back shook as he laughed. Jesse couldn't help laughing too. Rodge ignored them both.

"Well are we going to 'elp, or not?" Rodge said, his arms crossed.

"Yes, yes," Ian said, "I'll get you some shoes."

"Shoes?" Jesse asked.

Then Jesse watched as Ian climbed the nearest boojiegoojie tree, grabbed two of the dangling red fruits and threw them up to Rodge. Rodge caught them and then disappeared into his car. A few seconds later he stood up on the edge of the hot dog where he teetered for a moment before jumping over the side. Jesse cried out. But Rodge simply bounced up and down and up and down until he finally slowed to a stop. Jesse realized, with astonishment, that Rodge was wearing the red fruits over his feet like shoes.

"Boojiefruits," Rodge said, "the bounciest fruits on Foodie Island."

Ian handed Jesse two boojiefruits. "Don't put them on yet," he said, "first we need to find Fifine."

14
BOUNCING BOOJIEFRUITS

"Can you spot her again Rodge?" Ian asked.

Rodge began jumping and the boojiefruits bounced him higher and higher until he was above the tops of the trees. On one of his long bounces down he said, "I see 'er!"

"Does she see you?" Ian asked.

"Yes!" came Rodge's answer from way up high.

"Which way?" Ian asked.

"Walk straight ahead and then turn right at the edge o' the boojiegoojie trees," Rodge yelled.

Ian set off into the trees. Jesse followed, clutching his pair of boojiefruit shoes. They wound their way through the trees, pushing aside the hanging fruits and stepping over thick undergrowth. When Jesse reached out to push a small boojiefruit aside, it dropped into his hand. He looked at it then popped it into his mouth. It reminded him of a soft, chewy, cherry-flavored candy that he liked to eat at home. Only it tasted more vibrant, as though it were made from real, ripe cherries. He picked a few more as he walked. Some he ate and the others he stuffed into his pockets for later.

It felt like a long time, and Jesse wondered if they would ever get out of the trees. But finally, the path grew lighter and then he and Ian stood blinking in the sunshine.

"There she is," Ian said, pointing up toward a set of tall, brown cliffs to their right.

Jesse squinted his eyes. "I don't see anything." And then he saw it. Or he thought he saw it. Something pink flashed up on the rocks.

"Did you see that?" Ian asked, excited.

"Yeah, I think so."

"That's her basket liner."

"Her basket liner?"

"When Fifine goes out collecting flowers and herbs and things, she always lines her basket with a pink cloth." Ian ran closer to the cliffs. He cupped his hedgehog hands around his mouth and yelled, "FIFINE!"

"Yes, it is me!" they heard from above.

"I'm coming to rescue you!" Ian yelled. He pulled the red boojiefruits over his feet. Then he crouched like an athlete about to do the standing long jump, swung his arms back behind him, then forward and then back behind him again before jumping into the air. He rose a whole two inches off the ground. Jesse mentally noted that jumping was not a hedgesquirrel's strong point. But Ian continued undaunted, and twenty-six jumps later he reached the height of the outcropping of rock where they had seen Fifine's pink cloth. The only problem was that he couldn't jump forward onto the ledge because all of his effort was going up rather than out.

Jesse grasped the dilemma, stretched the red boojiefruits over his shoes, and started jumping next to Ian. It took considerable effort, but eventually their bounces synchronized. And at the top of the next coordinated bounce, Jesse pushed Ian onto the outcropping.

15
THE RESCUE

Jesse continued to bounce up and down. He watched Ian, after recovering from the surprise of being shoved in midair, locate Fifine cowering in a corner behind a large rock. She looked up at him and smiled weakly.

"I did not know I was so afraid of heights!" she said.

"Neither did I."

She gasped. "You are afraid too?"

"No, I mean…never mind. Are you alright?"

"I'm fine except for being twenty feet off the ground."

"How, or, why did you come up here?"

"You know I am a chef. Yes? Well, I came up here because I spied the very rare 'Joie de Jeanine' berry growing in a cleft of the Toffee Rocks. I found a pair of boojiefruit shoes, bounced up here, gathered some berries and then…became terrified."

"I have no idea what a Joie de Jeanine berry is, but I'd be delighted if you'd say it in your French accent about thirty-seven more times."

She looked up at him with a faint smile.

"How long have you been up here?"

"Two hours? Two days? I really don't know."

Ian picked up her basket full of berries. "I'll give these to Jesse and then come back for you."

"Jesse?"

"A friend." Ian walked back around the rock to find Jesse still bouncing, and grinning. He held the basket out. "Down please," he said, because he didn't have time to explain anything more. On Jesse's next bounce up he grabbed the basket.

Ian went back to Fifine who still crouched in the corner.

"How will I get down?" she asked.

"You're going to have to hold on, but carefully, so I don't poke you full of holes."

"Are you joking?"

"Perhaps, but there's only one way to find out."

Fifine looked up into Ian's grinning face.

"I think maybe you are teasing your poor friend."

He smiled gently, reassuringly. Then he pulled her by the hand to the edge of the rocks, scooped her into his arms and said, "Close your eyes!" before jumping into the air.

16
JOIE DE JEANINE PIE

Jesse watched Ian scoop a ball of fur into his arms before going over the edge. A screech pierced the air, followed by what sounded like a series of muffled mews. And then Ian stood still on the ground, unclasped his arms and an animal resembling a mix between a fox and a cat unfurled. She looked up at Ian with profound relief. Then she wrapped her arms around him and squeezed. When she let go, Ian looked down at the ground while readjusting his hat.

"I cannot thank you enough Ian!"

"Oh it was nothing."

"No, really, you must come to my house and I will bake you a Joie de Jeanine pie!"

Jesse had never heard of a Joie de Jeanine pie, but he wanted Fifine to say it about twenty-four more times.

"Please?" she said.

Ian, Jesse, Fifine and Fifine's basket went in Ian's scone. Rodge followed in his hot dog car. They drove back over the bridge, past the Brusselkale Forest, over the Choco River and past the grassy meadow. At the edge

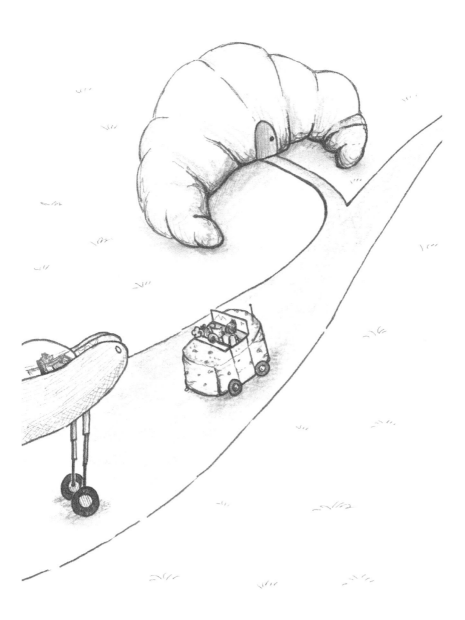

of the meadow sat the largest, flakiest croissant Jesse had ever seen.

"Your house?" he asked Fifine.

"But of course," she said smiling.

Ian pulled his scone up to a stop in front of the croissant. Rodge pulled alongside and yelled down, "I'm going back 'ome to work on the 'ydraulics."

"No pie?" Fifine asked.

"I'd love to," Rodge said, "but I've gotta get it ready for the big race."

"I'll save you a piece then," Fifine said smiling.

"Aww…you're too kind." And then, with a final wave, Rodge drove off.

"There's a race?" Jesse asked, looking at Ian.

"Aye, every year there's a big car race, but it's not for a couple weeks yet."

"Where's the racecourse?"

"The island is the racecourse, or at least, the main road around it."

"Wow! That sounds exciting. I'd love to see it!"

"It is exciting," Ian said, "and wild and exhilarating and, well…it's quite a race."

"Enough chitchat," Fifine said, "it's time for pie!" She linked her arms in theirs and led them into the house.

The inside of Fifine's croissant house was, much like Rodge's, light, airy and bright. Ian and Jesse waited in her living room. Jesse sat on a French roll chair which grew smaller and smaller as he continued to take bites out of it.

"Pretty soon you'll be sitting on a stool," Ian laughed.

Jesse grinned. "And your armchair seems to have lost its limbs."

They both laughed. Clattering noises came from the kitchen. Then a sweet aroma drifted into the living room. Fifine followed with two plates of pie, the inside of the pie a bright, shimmering pink.

Jesse took a bite and when the flavor hit his tongue, he closed his eyes. His parents sometimes did that when eating something they found particularly delicious and he had always wondered why. But now, he understood. The pie was *that* good.

"You like it?" Fifine asked Jesse, her eyes bright.

"This pie," Jesse said with his mouth full, "is the best pie I've ever tasted in my whole life."

Fifine smiled. "I am so glad. And you, Ian?"

"You never disappoint Fifine."

"Well then, perhaps my terrible experience on the Toffee Rocks is all worth it. A good chef goes to great lengths you know."

"Yes," said Ian, "but maybe good chefs can also have help."

"Are you offering?" Fifine asked.

"I'd be happy to," Ian said.

"Perfect!" Fifine clapped her hands. "The next time I go searching for Joie de Jeanine berries, I will find you."

Ian opened his mouth to respond and then fell off his chair. The chairs, the living room, the walls…the entire croissant was shaking. And Jesse, in a panic, tried to remember what to do in an earthquake.

17
AN EXPLOSION

Fifine and Ian looked at one another and both yelled, "Ooeygooeycheesakayummaooey!"

"Grab the chairs!" Fifine yelled.

Ian hoisted one onto his shoulder.

"You too, Jesse!" Ian said.

Jesse, confused, picked up the bread stool. "Shouldn't we…"

"Follow me!" Fifine raced out the door and across the meadow. Ian and Jesse followed, awkwardly clutching their chairs. Jesse saw other animals running. They also carried household items. He saw chairs, tables, baskets, pillows, picture frames and pendant lamps. He even saw two animals struggling with a desk. The ground still moved slightly, so that everyone lurched as they sped toward the meadow. Clutching, bumbling, and tripping, everyone ran.

When Fifine stopped, Jesse saw that she stood in front of a shallow ditch. Animals were lining up all along the ditch with their various house wares. They acted like nothing was wrong. The lack of concern perplexed Jesse. It was as though earthquakes happened all the time. And perhaps they did. Jesse couldn't possibly know. But as he pondered the possible reasons for their nonchalance, he heard a loud explosion.

Jesse dropped to the ground with his hands over his head. He lay still for a few moments before daring to move. He looked up. No one else seemed the least bit perturbed. In fact, they all continued chatting, laughing and setting up lawn chairs. If Jesse didn't know better he would think they were preparing for a party and not experiencing a natural disaster. And then he saw it.

It started as a thin yellow stream, but quickly grew into a river that filled the ditch almost to the top. When the animals first saw it they let out a collective cheer. And then Jesse watched in fascination as they began to break apart all the various household items they had toted to the ditch's edge.

"Here," said Fifine, handing Jesse a piece of French roll.

"What do I…"

"Dip it," she said, "like this." And then he watched as she dipped her piece of bread into the yellow river and popped it into her mouth. "Fondue," she said. "Try it!"

Jesse dipped his bread into the cheese and took a bite.

"Do you like it?" Fifine asked.

"It's incredible!" he said. "How did it get here?"

"From the volcano," Ian said, "Ooegooeycheesakayummaooey. And when she blows, she flows."

"Does it happen every day?" Jesse asked, dipping more bread into the river of cheese.

"Oh no," said Fifine, "We never know when she's going to blow, but we never want to miss it."

"I can believe that!" Jesse said, smiling. He looked up and down the ditch. Everyone was dunking something into the river; chair legs, sofa cushions, fence posts and tabletops. Jesse even saw a badger-like animal dip a small wheelbarrow into the cheese which she then fed to all six of her children. A festive air ran up and down the ditch as families and friends and neighbors feasted together. Jesse caught sight of Rodge, farther up the river, dunking a license plate. Jesse waved and Rodge waved back with a grin.

Jesse grabbed another chunk of bread and then stopped when he heard a faint buzzing noise. He tried to think where he had heard it before. The noise grew. He crinkled his forehead in thought. And then there it was in front of him; a zipzap, with its rainbow coloring, spinning helicopter blades and large goggles. In its mouth it carried a yamzirdle flower. It hovered next to Jesse, blinking its wide eyes.

"For me?" Jesse asked.

The zipzap nodded. Jesse reached out and took the yellow goblet-like flower from the bird.

"Thank you," he said.

The bird zipped away. When Jesse looked at Fifine and Ian, he saw that they both held flowers as well.

"They're so quiet," Jesse said. He looked out and saw hundreds of zipzaps carrying yamzirdle flowers and weaving their way among the animals.

"They're interesting animals," Ian said, "They can go from silent to deafening in about five seconds."

"Sounds like my baby sister," Jesse laughed. And then he thought of Avery and Zack and his mom and dad. He swallowed hard. He looked down into his goblet. Bubbles rose to the surface and then instead of popping, floated into the air. Jesse, his eyes still prickling from emotion, reached out to pop one.

18
HOME AGAIN

Jesse felt himself somersaulting. The faces of Fifine and Ian appeared then disappeared then appeared again. They looked concerned. They were pointing at him. And they were huge. He looked down at himself. Tiny legs, tiny feet…he was in a bubble again! It started to lift into the air. Fifine and Ian watched in dismay as he floated higher and higher. He smiled to reassure them. Then as a breeze blew from the west, he waved and yelled, "Goodbye! Goodbye!"

A zipzap, which looked a lot like the one he first saw on S'more Beach, flew up beside him. Jesse waved to it from the bubble. The bird looked at him with its huge goggle eyes and smiled shyly. It flew next to Jesse until the ocean changed from a turquoise blue to a deep navy. And then, after a nod, it sped back towards the island.

Jesse watched it go with some regret. He enjoyed floating next to the funny little bird. Turning around he looked back at the island. It was only a small speck now. The wind continued to push him east over the wide, wide ocean. He floated over a cruise ship, its decks dotted with people, and then a fishing boat with its nets trailing behind.

In time, on the horizon, other specks came into view. And his heart leapt when he recognized the shape of the harbor, the familiar bobbing boats and the skyline of downtown.

"Hi, harbor!" he yelled, "Hi, boats! Hi, downtown!" He laughed with sheer joy. Then he floated over an office building and yelled, "Hi, Dad's office!"

The bubble sailed past downtown and over the sprawling zoo.

"Hey gorillas, look at me!" Jesse waved excitedly, "Ooh, ooh, eeh, eeh!"

Soon Jesse floated over the freeway, the university and then finally over even more familiar landmarks; the grocery store, the post office and yes, his house. The bubble hung suspended above his house for a moment before floating down and down and down. It felt like forever. When he finally neared the kitchen window, a sudden breeze blew him into the house. Jesse drifted over the kitchen sink and down to the floor where the bubble popped.

Jesse stood looking at the kitchen in amazement. Everything looked the same. He turned to the sink full of soapy water and realized it still had Avery's plate in it. The other plates, stacked next to the sink, still had pasta and marinara sauce residue on them. They were the same dishes he had been washing when he left!

"Weird," Jesse said to himself. Had it all been a dream? Or some weird kind of daydream?

"Hey," Zack said, breathless from running inside, "are you finished yet? Dad and I are playing soccer and we want you to play too!"

"I...I...I'm not quite done...I...," Jesse stammered. Then he grabbed Zack and gave him a hug. "I missed you little buddy."

"Are you okay?" Zack asked looking up at Jesse.

"Yeah, I...I'll be out in a minute."

"Okay!" Zack ran back outside.

Jesse loaded the dishwasher. Then his mother walked into the kitchen.

"Oh Mom, it's so good to see you!"

"Is it?" she laughed. "You haven't seen me for a full ten minutes."

"Ten minutes? That's it?"

"Yeah." She laughed again.

"Well...it felt longer, that's all."

"You're sweet Jesse. And a great kid. Thanks for doing the dishes." She gave him a hug.

"Can I go outside and play now?"

"Yes, you may."

Jesse gave her a wide smile then ran out the back door to join his father and brother.

But as he ran down the porch steps, he noticed his shoes and stopped short. Covering his blue cross-trainers, because he had forgotten to take them off, was a pair of red, shining, boojiefruits.

THE END

APPENDICES
(EXTRA STUFF)

THE HOW-TO-UNDERSTAND RODGE GUIDE

'ad – had

anyfing – anything

'appy – happy

'ard – hard

'ave – have

'aven't – haven't

chasin' – chasing

drivin' – driving

'ealth – health

'eard – heard

'eart – heart

eatin' – eating

'elp – help

'em – them

'er - her

'ere – here

everfing – everything

fing – thing

fink – think

finkin' – thinking

frostin' – frosting

gettin' – getting

growin' – growing

'ide – hide

'im – him

makin' – making

mum - mom

o' – of

'ome – home

'opefully – hopefully

'ot dog – hot dog

'ouse – house

'ow – how

'owever – however

prattlin' – prattling

ramblin' – rambling

seein' – seeing

settlin' – settling

sloggin' – slogging

soft'earted – softhearted

somefing' – something

steerin' – steering

takin' – taking

'umdrum – humdrum

'undred – hundred

'ungry – hungry

winnin' – winning

wiv - with

wivout – without

workin' – working

'ydraulics – hydraulics

RODGE'S RIDICULOUS RHYMES

Muffin Top

My car it drives wiv a toot, toot, toot!
It's a blueberry muffin jam packed wiv fruit.
The top's the best so I eat it all off,
Then I swallow lots o' bugs 'til it makes me cough.
The bugs 'ave protein makin' me so strong;
I can feel my muscles growin' all day long.
Convertible cars are the best you see
They give you free food and a buff body!

S'more Beach

Pull up a boulder. Take a bite.
We might stay right 'ere all night.
Roast a mallow, grab a cracker -
Make a triple decked out stacker.
Ooey gooey oh so yummy,
Settlin' warmly in your tummy.

Ode to a Carrot Ginger Cupcake

Oh cupcake that does so sweetly shine,
Above the crumbly cliffs that I must climb.
You make my 'eart strong and my arteries too,
Who knew all the great things that you could do!

ABOUT THE AUTHOR

Dana Ryan is the author of the *Martín y Pepe* series of easy reader Spanish books. She lives with her husband and three children in Southern California where she enjoys being outdoors, cooking and eating really good food.

Made in United States
North Haven, CT
20 September 2022